Addison Addley

AND THE THINGS THAT AREN'T THERE

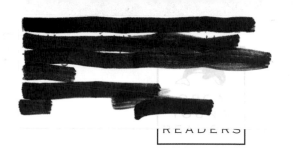

READERS

Addison Addley

AND THE THINGS THAT AREN'T THERE

MELODY DEFIELDS
McMILLAN

ORCA BOOK PUBLISHERS

Library and Archives Canada Cataloguing in Publication

McMillan, Melody DeFields, 1956-
Addison Addley and the Things that Aren't There / written by Melody DeFields McMillan.

(Orca young readers)
ISBN 978-1-55143-949-5

I. Title. II. Series.

PS8625.M54A64 2008   jC813'.6   C2007-906964-9

First published in the United States, 2008
Library of Congress Control Number: 2007940947

Summary: Addison has to give a speech at school, but he'd
rather be fishing or playing baseball than writing.

Orca Book Publishers gratefully acknowledges the support for its publishing programs
provided by the following agencies: the Government of Canada through the Book
Publishing Industry Development Program and the Canada Council for the Arts,
and the Province of British Columbia through the BC Arts Council
and the Book Publishing Tax Credit.

Typesetting by Bruce Collins
Cover artwork by Peter Ferguson
Author photo by Justin McMillan

ORCA BOOK PUBLISHERS
PO Box 5626, STN. B
VICTORIA, BC CANADA
V8R 6S4

ORCA BOOK PUBLISHERS
PO Box 468
CUSTER, WA USA
98240-0468

www.orcabook.com
Printed and bound in Canada.

11 10 09 08 • 5 4 3 2

To Taryn and Justin

Acknowledgments

Thanks to my editor, Sarah Harvey, for all her help.

Chapter One

I hate doing speeches. I hate doing speeches more than I hate being the skinniest guy on the baseball team. Just because my name is Addison, everyone thinks I should be smart or something. Maybe they're confusing me with Edison, the inventor of the light bulb. Maybe they think that my yellow hair sends some sort of weird Vitamin C energy to my brain. I don't know.

My name may be smart, but I'm sure not. Not at school stuff, anyway. I could be, my teacher tells me, if I would "apply" myself. Apply myself to what? It sounds like I need a giant tube of glue.

"Now, Addison," I can hear her say, "if only you would apply yourself, you'd grasp fractions in no time at all."

Now I can think of a lot of things I'd like to grasp, like maybe the controller for my new video game or the reel of my old fishing pole, but fractions aren't on the list. Besides, who would want to be an expert on fractions anyway? They're useless except for the odd saying like *I'm halfway done my ice cream* or *If I had half a brain, I'd be able to come up with a topic for my speech.*

That's what I was thinking about on Saturday morning. If I had half a brain, I'd be able to come up with some incredible idea that would stun all the other kids in my grade five class, I thought. Heck, I'd even settle for a quarter of a brain. It's not that I don't have much of a brain. It's just that I choose not to waste my brain on school stuff. Personally, I think I've got more common sense than anybody I know, except for the guy at the gas station where I buy my worms. He's got to be pretty smart to make people pay for those slimy creatures. I'd probably make a great worm seller.

If I could think of a really great topic, I might be able to just make up the speech right while I was saying it. No sense wasting energy, I told myself as I brushed my teeth. Let me get that straight. I wasn't really brushing them, just giving them a quick scrape and then pretending they were clean. Sometimes I just let the water run and then I spit as loudly as I can into the sink to make it sound like I'm brushing them. I always pay for it at the next trip to the dentist though. Things have a disgusting way of catching up to you. In the back of my mind I knew I should be brushing longer. But that's where the thought usually stays—in the very back of my mind, where it belongs. This was definitely going to be a quick-scrape day.

I spit one more time and closed my eyes, trying to force a quarter of my brain into action.

"Breakfast!" Mom called from downstairs.

Saved by the yell. That was enough work for now anyway. Little did I know that by the time breakfast was over, I'd have my incredible topic. And how was I to know that, like dirty teeth, fractions have a disgusting way of catching up to you?

Chapter Two

"What's up?" I asked as I caught the piece of French toast that came flying through the kitchen doorway. Mom sometimes goes crazy in the kitchen. If she doesn't get to cook a big meal for a couple of days, she saves up all her energy and throws it into the food. Once she made three different salads, four kinds of sandwiches and two types of pudding, all for my lunch and all in ten minutes. I bet she could make breakfast, lunch and dinner all at once, in between rearranging the kitchen furniture.

Saturdays were French toast days. French toast days were sometimes good, sometimes bad. It all depended on what wacky health-food-store ingredients Mom had decided to use that day. Last week it was honey and alfalfa sprouts—definitely not a good day. The week before it was organic sunflower with burnt crusts. I'm not sure if the burnt crusts were organic or not.

This week looked better. There seemed to be almonds and cherries flattened into the bread. At least I hoped they were cherries. They might have been kidney beans. With my mom you never know.

"What's the big rush?" I asked as I watched her throw another piece into the frying pan.

"It's the big astronomy event today," she said between gulps of organic papaya juice.

Now, I might not know much about science, but I was pretty sure that the stars came out at night, not at eight o'clock in the morning.

"Ah, Mom…I think that maybe you've got your times mixed up," I offered helpfully. Mom sometimes gets confused. I remember once when she showed up at the baseball field with five dozen carob chip and apple muffins. That was really nice of her and all, but completely unnecessary. Our team wasn't even playing that day. It was the firefighters' guinea pig races instead. I guess I forgot to mention to her that our tournament had been postponed. The firefighters liked the muffins though. I think the guinea pigs did too. If we ever have a fire, I bet the trucks will get to our house really fast.

Mom looked flushed for a minute, as if she actually believed me for once, but then she suddenly remembered.

"No, no, no. We're driving to Williamstown to look at the new observatory. We're eating lunch at the Galaxy restaurant. Then we're having a meeting to discuss the election of officers next month. I would die to be the treasurer."

I looked at Mom to see if she was sick. She looked fine but I couldn't be sure. She'd been trying to keep really busy lately. Maybe she was too busy to think straight. Since she and Dad got divorced four years ago, she had tried at least eight different clubs. First she'd tried belly dancing. Next it was bread making. Then came basket weaving. I guess that was so she'd have something to put the bread in. Herb drying, yoga, Japanese gardening, Chinese lantern making and Greek cooking rounded out the list. I had used my calculator to figure out that was two clubs a year. She usually quit after a couple of months, but maybe this one would stick.

But treasurer? It was a mystery to me why anyone would want to do a job without getting paid, especially a job involving numbers. Come to think of it, I didn't really get what was so exciting about staring at a bunch of stars.

"Why do you like looking at stars so much?" I asked as I picked the almonds out of the toast and stuffed them in my pocket. The squirrels would like them better than I did. I had to do my part for animal welfare. I always leave the garage window open a crack just in case the bats need someplace to sleep. Mom's not real keen on that one. She didn't really like the toad house I built out of her new bamboo placemats either.

Mom looked at me like I came from Mars, which I'm sure she hopes to see at the astronomy club.

"How could you not like looking at the stars?" she asked, shooting me a look that said I must have been adopted. "I love the stars. And I want to be the treasurer because it's a way of meeting people," she explained. "I don't think I stand much of a chance because the only experience I have working with numbers, in an official sense, was when I volunteered with the humane society. I had to collect and record the donations we received for the feed-a-kitten day. I don't think that kitten food expenses are in the same category as big telescope expenses, but I'm going to try anyway," she said happily.

"Besides, you know I love working with numbers," she added, staring at me in a way that made me feel like I was supposed to share her feelings. I think Mom secretly wanted to be an accountant or some other strange math-loving creature. She was always trying to play little number games with me, like telling me to see if I could balance my bank account before the computer did it for me. She didn't know that I just kept the money from my paper route in my underwear drawer, between all my holey socks. That was enough balancing for me. She even used to make number-shaped cookies to try to get me to add as I was eating. Instead of putting the two and the three cookies together like she suggested, I just ate the whole plateful. I figured that was the quickest—and tastiest—way to get to five.

She downed her raspberry tea in a single gulp. "Did you know," she said, "that those stars that you're talking about actually made that starlight thousands of years ago? It's taken many years to reach us."

"So that's what you see when you look up there, some really old light?" I asked.

"No, that's just it," Mom explained, practically glowing now. "It's what you don't see."

I scratched my head as I put my French toast into the microwave to warm up. I was sure I was adopted now. Either that or I took after Dad. He lived in Australia now, trying out a new career as a sheep farmer. He probably didn't have time to look at the sky, just the fields. Besides, I bet the stars were upside down in Australia. I knew he didn't like numbers. I guess he didn't like letters either, since he'd only sent us two e-mails in the last year.

"There are so many unexplained mysteries out there," Mom gushed as she threw the frying pan into the sink. "If it takes that long for starlight to reach us, don't you wonder what those stars look like right now? We see a star—but maybe it's something else by now and we won't know for thousands of years. We see what that star looked like way back then. Because it's so far away, it takes ages for the information on what it looks like now to reach us. Who knows? It might not even be there anymore. Scientists are constantly discovering things like new planets and asteroids or discovering that things they thought were planets aren't really planets after all. Not everything is as it appears."

"I see," I said.

"What about black holes?" she continued. Her face lit up like the night sky. "Black holes are really dense areas in the universe that have such a strong gravitational field that nothing can escape from them, not even light. Everything just disappears into them. You can't see them, so you can't prove they exist. That's what some people think, anyway. But you can't prove that they don't exist either. Like I said before, just because you can't see something, it doesn't mean it isn't there."

She blew me a kiss as she breezed out the door.

The microwave beeped. I stared at it for a minute. Then I got that flash of inspiration that sometimes comes my way. I had a topic for my speech, and it was sweet.

Chapter Three

"Things that aren't there. Are you crazy?" Sam asked that afternoon as he helped me deliver the Saturday papers. My best friend sometimes thinks the worst of me. Maybe that means my worst enemy sometimes thinks the best of me. That would be nice. Sam snorted like he always does when he doesn't approve of my undeniably brilliant plans. I remember the time that he didn't believe me when I came up with this fantastic idea of how to get a day off school to go to the fair across the road. All we had to do was convince Principal Pierce that we were doing an art project. We needed to take a picture looking down at the school-yard filled with kids at recess. It had to be taken from a high point, like, say, a Ferris wheel. We couldn't wait until the weekend because there'd be no kids in the yard then. The trouble was, Principal Pierce didn't believe me either. He made us take the picture from his second-story office window.

Sam shook his head. "Why don't you pick a normal topic, like the history of industrialization?" he suggested.

Now it was my turn to snort. Normal? The history of industrialization hardly sounded normal. I didn't even know what it meant. Sam always used big words. The problem was, he usually knew what they meant too. Why Sam had to be so smart, I don't know. I guess it was so I could look dumber. He's a thoughtful guy.

I explained about starlight and black holes and Mom and the astronomy club. "There have to be lots of things that aren't there," I said. "Like this morning, when I heard the microwave beep. I couldn't see those waves, but my French toast was hot, so they must have been there. I could just call my speech 'Things That Are There But You Can't See Them,' but that's too boring. My title's better. Besides, a hundred years ago, people wouldn't have believed that something as weird as a microwave really was there. It would have been a thing that's not there back then. I bet there are some things that aren't there today, but in fifty years from now, they will be."

I was proud of myself. I'd come up with that one pretty fast.

Sam was quiet for a minute and then he spun around.

"Things that aren't there!" he cried. "I get it now! You mean like how dogs can hear a whistle at really high frequencies even though we can't? We'd never know that whistle was there, but the dog sure does. Things that aren't there, they're just not there. Not there." Sam always repeats things three times when he gets excited or nervous. "At least to some of us. This has merit," he practically shouted. "This could be good," he translated for me.

"Like I said, this speech is going to be good. It will practically write itself," I boasted. It's hard to be humble when you come up with a really good idea. The problem was, I couldn't seem to come up with any more of them. I couldn't write a speech on just one or two things that weren't there. I needed more.

"How about UFOs?" Sam said, looking up at the sky. "So many people believe in them, but they can't prove they exist. They're not there, or…are they?"

I wasn't sure I wanted someone to prove UFOs were there, thanks just the same. Ever since I'd watched that movie about a giant football with lights landing in someone's backyard, I had tried to avoid the subject. I'd had nightmares for weeks. If there really were UFOs, I didn't want to know about them. Let them stay where they were.

I slapped Sam on the back. "Just keep thinking," I encouraged him. There was no use putting my brain to work when Sam could come up with the ideas for me. You know, energy conservation and all. I had to do my bit.

Besides, Sam had his speech on medieval times already written and probably memorized. I needed to concentrate on bigger things, like how I was going to help Mom become the treasurer of the astronomy club. After all, if it wasn't for her, I wouldn't have my incredible speech idea. I told Sam that if he could concentrate on my speech for a while, then I could concentrate on helping Mom. Two heads are better than one.

I hadn't seen Mom so excited in a long time. The way I figured, if she could get out and spend her time worrying about somebody else's money, she wouldn't have so much time to worry about what I was doing with mine. She'd have to expend all her worrying energy at the club. Heck, she'd probably even enjoy not having as much time to tell me to clean my room, and she might not notice when I stashed peas in the crack under the table so I wouldn't have to eat them. If I could help her out, I'd be glad to do it.

It was sort of nice being around her when she was really happy. She always had a goofy faraway look on her face, as if she was imagining that she was on the moon. Sometimes I'd catch her humming something that I remembered from a long time ago when I was a little kid. It didn't matter that it was out of tune. It sure beat listening to the sound of her crying.

The astronomy board needed to find out about Mom's talents. She knew how to change the oil in the car. She was good at hammering nails and flipping over cards with one finger, but I doubted those skills would help. She could wake up at the same time every morning without even using an alarm clock, but that was no good because the club met at night.

She was a real genius at math. She could add up the number of times I didn't do my homework last year without even using a calculator. Let me tell you, that's a lot of adding. She could also multiply anything by 365 and come up with the right answer. That's how she figured out how many times last year she had to remind me to shut the door and wipe my shoes. It was three or four times a day times 365.

Yep, I'd figure out something. Busy as I was, I'd find a way to get Mom elected. Some people just can't do things without my help, even if they won't admit it. Anyway, finding a sneaky way to turn the tables in Mom's favor was a whole lot more interesting than writing a speech. That could be Sam's job.

Sam was smack in the middle of a good thought when we rounded the corner of Pine Street and ran right into the Lamp. I don't mean the streetlight. I mean Tiffany Wilson, the Lamp for short. That's what my great-aunt's old kitchen lamp is called. A Tiffany lamp. It's got a huge, colorful glass shade on it that looks too big for the bulb. Mom says it's really old and valuable. It just plain looks too big to me. Tiffany is the meanest girl in grade five. Heck, I take that back. Tiffany is the meanest girl in the school. Whoever said that girls can't be as mean as guys sure didn't know Tiffany.

"Well, if it isn't Sam the geek and his stupid friend Add, or is it Odd?" the Lamp sneered as she and her friends strutted toward us.

Now I don't mind being called stupid, but I hate being called Add by people like her. It's okay for Sam to call me that. That's best friend sort of stuff.

She stepped closer. Tiffany wasn't really fat. She just had this dumb way of puffing her shoulders out and prancing like a peacock to make herself look important. The only thing she looked was weird. Her hair was frizzy and so big that it looked like she was wearing a lampshade. A Tiffany lampshade.

"Shut up, Tiffany," I said. "Go back where you came from."

"Hi, Tiffany," Sam said, pushing his glasses up his sweaty nose. "Add and I were just discussing our speech topics, our topics, our speeches."

NO!! I screamed silently to Sam. Don't tell her! I don't know why Sam always tries to be nice to mean people like the Lamp. The nicer he is to her, the meaner she'll be to him because she knows she can get away with it. He just doesn't get it.

"Oh, I can't wait to hear this one," Tiffany purred. "Let me guess—'The Stupider Side of Stupid.' Am I close? Or is it 'The Dumber Side of Dumb'?"

Close enough for me to shove you into that puddle, I thought. Sam could read my mind. "Be careful," he whispered. "Her mother is the president of the astronomy club. You want your mom to get on the board, right?"

I groaned. Not only was the astronomy club weird, but it had annoying people running it. I knew Tiffany's mother, and she was just as annoying as Tiffany. That would definitely make my job a lot harder. I'd have to have a word with Mom so she could straighten out her priorities. You've gotta look at the big picture. Why would you want to join a club where you'd be around such annoying people? A nice harmless club would be better. Take the knitting club, for example. Sam's grandmother ran that one. You couldn't get any more harmless than her.

Sam stepped toward Tiffany. "Things that aren't there," he said happily. "You get it? Things that aren't there, but they might be."

Tiffany stared at us with her eyes bulging out of her big head.

"Things that aren't there!" she snorted. Then she choked. Her shiny red face screwed up into a big question mark.

Her friends giggled. "Look, Add," she said. "We know you're stupid, but this is stupid even for you. What do you mean, things that aren't there?"

I'd had enough. "Well, here's a starter," I said. "Things that aren't there. Number one…your brain!"

Tiffany's face turned even redder. "Things that aren't there," she sputtered. "Number two…the favorite speech trophy. It's sure not going to be there in your hands with such a stupid topic!" She stormed away.

I'd forgotten about that trophy. If I had doubts about being able to come up with enough ideas for my speech topic, they were gone now. I decided that if Tiffany thought my topic was a bad idea, then it probably was a good one. I was going to win that trophy. I may not know a lot of things, but I sure know how to be stubborn.

Chapter Four

On Monday at school, Miss Steane told us more about the speech trophy. It was donated by good old Mrs. Wilson, the Lamp's mother. She was always getting her nose into school stuff. It wouldn't be hard to do, because her nose was so big. No wonder Tiffany wanted to win that trophy so badly. She probably picked it out herself.

"Now, this isn't going to be a popularity contest," Miss Steane explained firmly in her teacher voice. Miss Steane was great. Sometimes she used a normal human voice and sometimes a teacher voice. She was really talented. She always seemed to know what we were going to say even before we said it. I guess I've told her too many times that the dog ate my homework because by now she knows I don't even have a dog, and she won't let me finish my excuse. I'll have to come up with a different one, like the squirrels used my homework pages to build their nest. The best thing about Miss Steane was that she was fair. She didn't treat the smart kids better than the rest of us. She'd only been teaching for a couple of years, but she was the best teacher we'd ever had.

"Public speaking is an art," she explained. "Not only do we gain knowledge from the speaker, but, ideally, we'll be entertained. After all, in the real world, if a speech or presentation to a company is boring, it's not going to make an impact. We're not going to make a sale or convince a board to vote for us."

I caught the last few words as I studied the eraser on my pencil. I wondered how many pieces I could chew off before it was even with the metal top. I like doing things like that. Experimenting with science and all. The world always needs new ideas. I like to help out. Once I even tried to invent my own paper shredder. I figured we had too many old bills lying around the house. Mom always cried when she looked at them. I taped a cheese grater onto the wheel of Mom's exercise bike; then I made paper airplanes out of the bills and threw them at the spokes while Sam pedalled. It sure clogged up the spokes of that old bike, but it didn't work very well as a shredder. I'll have to try that one again and have Sam pedal faster.

"Did you hear what I said, Addison?" Miss Steane asked.

"Ah, sure, we have to convince the board to vote for us," I said. Just like I'd have to somehow convince the astronomy club board to vote for Mom. She'd never be able to do it on her own. Maybe I could trick Mrs. Wilson into believing that Mom had been abducted by aliens once and that now she knew everything about life on other planets. I'd tell her that Mom could list all the space movies ever made. Heck, she could probably even list all the characters in all the space movies ever made.

"Right, something like that," Miss Steane said. She switched to her normal voice.

"In other words," she continued, "let's liven things up. We don't want this to be a boring assignment. Have a bit of fun with it. That way, hopefully, no one has to be nervous."

That was a lot easier said than done. We only had one week until we started giving our speeches. Sam had told me that almost everyone already had theirs memorized. I hadn't even written mine yet. I kind of have this habit of putting things off until the last minute. Things turn out better that way. I think. Like the time I returned a new video game to the corner store just at the last minute. It was due at noon. I got to the door at 11:59. Good thing I did. If I had been there any earlier, I might have ended up in jail. It turns out that Sam's grandma had accidentally let her dog loose in the store. He'd knocked over two racks of potato chips and three jars of jelly beans. I don't think I would have been able to resist taking some free samples off the floor if I'd been there. Then I might have gotten arrested. Yep, being there just at the last minute worked for me that day.

Miss Steane smiled. "After the speeches are over on Wednesday, we're going to have a 'speeches are over, middle of the week' party. We'll present the favorite speech trophy and have some food and games. Don't forget; try to make your speech entertaining. We'll all vote for our favorite speech right before the party."

Everyone volunteered to bring stuff. I was going to bring the almonds from the stash I had stored for the squirrels, but I decided not to. The squirrels deserved them. When I found out Mrs. Wilson was organizing the party, I knew what I had to do. Mrs. Wilson was on the astronomy board. Mrs. Wilson loved to cook and eat. She also loved to try new recipes. Mrs. Wilson needed to find out about Mom's prize-winning healthy cooking. Well, maybe not prize-winning, but incredibly healthy.

That was my plan. I'd impress her with Mom's famous organic fruit punch. Technically it was called a fruit smoothie, but I preferred to call it punch. Smoothie sounds too much like baby food. Mrs. Wilson would be begging for the recipe and then begging my mom for more ideas. She'd vote for Mom for sure. I just love the way things fall into place sometimes. But I couldn't put my plan into action right away. I had more important things to do. It was Monday afternoon and that meant fishing. The creek is deserted on Monday afternoons. The fish like it that way. They like us too; we hadn't caught anything in two years. They were safe with us.

Sam was hopping up and down when I met him after school. He held open a battered old book from the library.

"Atoms," he said.

"Adam's what?" I asked. I didn't even know an Adam, except for the short guy on the baseball team last year.

"Atoms—like in science. They're the smallest thing you can imagine. Scientists base a lot of physics theories on them, but you can't see them, not even with a microscope. They think they're there because of the reactions of the stuff around them. An atom is a thing that isn't there, but it really is."

Sam looked proud of himself. "Wormholes," he said triumphantly.

Sam was thinking too much. We didn't have to dig wormholes; we were buying bait at the store. I tapped him on the shoulder. "Look," I pointed out. "We don't have shovels. We're buying our worms today, remember?"

"Wormholes, like in astronomy. Your mom would like this one. Some people believe that there are these things called wormholes. They're like invisible passageways to different parts of the universe and different times, sort of like time traveling. You can't see them, but you can't really prove they don't exist. They're things that aren't there."

"Whatever," I said, pretending to understand. Sam had worms on the brain, but I decided to write down those two ideas anyway. Even stupid ideas were better than none at this point.

As we walked into the gas station to get the worms, I saw Tiffany's older sister, Jennifer, behind the counter. I'd had enough of the Wilsons today, so I tried to get out of there quickly. Sam paid for the worms and I paid for the Popsicles we needed to keep up our energy. I handed Jennifer the exact change.

Or so I thought.

"Thanks for the tip, Addison," Jennifer said with a sickening smile. She was pretending to be sweet, but a sour candy would be sweeter.

I must have added wrong, as usual, because what should have been $1.38 suddenly became $1.83 in my head. I had given her too much. Like I said, I'm not too good at adding. Sometimes those dumb numbers just sneak into the wrong place.

Sam pushed me out the door before I could grab back my money.

"Remember the astronomy meeting and your mom," he whispered. "Remember Mrs. Wilson is on the board. Try to be nice."

I would rather be nice to a tarantula, but I thought I'd better take Sam's advice, for Mom's sake.

We reached the stream and divided the worms in half. Well, Sam did anyway. Did I already mention that

I'm not too good at dividing? I plopped my half of the worms into my hat. I always let Sam keep his worms in the carton because I'm a nice guy.

I tried to come up with ideas for my speech. I fished and I thought. I thought and I fished. Some days, the fish just aren't biting. Some days, neither are the ideas.

Chapter Five

That night I had nightmares. I mean, really gross nightmares. I was being chased by Tiffany, who didn't have a head anymore. That was good in a way because I didn't have to look at her face, but it was also bad because where her face should have been was a rotten fish head. She had a backup army of UFOs behind her, and the aliens, who all had fish heads, were shooting calculators at me. Some things are better left undreamt.

I woke up in a sweat when the phone rang beside my head. I looked at the clock. It was three o'clock in the morning.

I grabbed the phone, my heart still pounding from that dumb dream. "Hello?" I said, wishing the shadows by the closet didn't look quite so creepy.

"Ghosts," I heard someone breathe into the receiver.

I almost dropped the phone, but then I heard the word "ghosts" two more times. Two plus one equals three. That much I know. It had to be three-peater Sam.

"What the heck are you trying to do—give me a heart attack?" I half yelled. I didn't want to wake up Mom in the downstairs bedroom.

"Ghosts. They might be there with you right now," Sam said.

Great. I really needed to hear that. Suddenly that downstairs room looked good.

"Knock it off!" I said. "I'm trying to sleep."

"So many people believe in ghosts," Sam explained in a whisper. "Some people claim they've actually seen them, but there is no way of proving it. Some people hear them or just feel them. They are things that aren't there. Or are they?"

I'd rather not think about that right now, thank you very much, I thought. My teeth started chattering. I was sure it was from the cold.

"Yeah, thanks for your great idea, Sam. Let me sleep on it," I lied. There was no way in the world I was going to be able to go back to sleep now.

I turned on all the lights in my room and flipped the TV on low. I might as well put the time to good use, I reasoned. I took out my pad of paper and added "Ghosts" to my list.

Things That Aren't There
1. Tiffany's brain
2. Science stuff—microwaves, atoms
3. Dog whistles
4. UFOS
5. Astronomy stuff—black holes and wormholes
6. Ghosts

I stretched my brain as far as it could go and all I could come up with was one more thing.

7. An A on my speech

Chapter Six

It was a few days before I had to talk to Tiffany again. Miss Steane had told us the order of our speeches. I was scheduled to go last on Wednesday, the last day. I told you Miss Steane was the best. She probably knew I still hadn't written a word. I was starting to get a bit panicky about it, but I was sure I could pull it off. I still had a week. Good things come to those who wait, someone smart—maybe my dad—once said. I was really good at waiting. As long as it meant putting off work.

The Lamp cornered me at recess. I tried to hide behind Sam but she caught me anyway.

"Well, Oddison," she purred. She must spend her time making up stupid nicknames for me. I guess she's got nothing better to do.

"How's your speech going? What was it again? Let me see…things that aren't there. What a stupid, stupid topic."

"Yeah, well you're going to wish you weren't there when everyone laughs at your speech," I answered back. "What is it again—the history of lampshades?"

"You make me sick. I'm doing a speech on politeness—something you know nothing about," she sneered. "You present on Wednesday—that's only one week away. One week—that's seven days, in case you don't know how to count." Her little group of followers laughed.

I knew how to count all right. I'd count to ten. That would give me enough time to cool off. I thought of Tiffany's mother and the astronomy election. It only took me to seven to get back in control. "Things that aren't there," I said nice and calmly. "The fight that you're trying to pick with me. It's not going to work. It's just not there."

I was proud of myself. Tiffany has a way of getting under my skin, just like worm dirt gets under my fingernails. I'm lucky with the dirt because it washes right out. I wish I could say the same for Tiffany.

Chapter Seven

The next morning we had a chapter review on fractions. I don't know why they call it a review. Review means to go over something you already know, like reviewing the seven steps you need to take to get to the dragon in my favorite video game, or going over every flavor of ice cream three times before deciding on which one to get. I don't mind reviewing my game plan to become a famous inventor some day. But I definitely couldn't review fractions because I didn't understand them in the first place.

Besides, everybody knew that "review" was just a fancy word for "test." Teachers thought they could get away with sneaking one in if they called it something different.

I stared at the numbers on the page.

1/3 + 1/3 =

Did that equal 1/6? Or 2/3? Or 2 1/3? The only number that I was sure about was the zero I was going to get on that review.

That night I started writing my speech. I quit after ten minutes. I'd done quite a bit for one night. I had written two lines and I didn't want to burn out. I needed to pace myself.

Miss Steane, honorable judges, and fellow classmates,
Do you ever wonder if something is really there?

I put away my speech and headed downstairs to get something to eat. Writing works up an appetite. I grabbed some pita bread stuffed with meatless meat left over from supper. I threw out the meatless meat and stuffed the pita with peanut butter. No use wasting the good stuff on me.

Mom was out on the deck looking at the stars. She was holding up one hand with her fingers spread out. It looked like she was trying to put a spell on the sky.

"What are you doing?" I asked her as I jumped into my old hammock under the pine tree that overhung the deck.

"I'm trying to measure the distance between the stars," she said, passing me a plate of flaxseed and honey cookies. "Did you know that if you hold your hand outstretched like this, the span from your thumb to your little finger is about twenty-five degrees, which is the length of the Big Dipper?" she asked.

I nodded, pretending to be interested. I picked the flaxseeds out of the cookies and dropped them through the holes in the deck for the birds. "Don't you think you should be using something better to look at the stars with than your fingers?" I asked. It looked pretty weird to me, like some voodoo thing that I'd seen on TV.

"Sure, a telescope would be nice," Mom said. "Maybe if we had a little more money to spare we could look into buying a used one."

Or maybe she could borrow one from the astronomy club if she got elected, I thought. Heck, maybe she could borrow one for me too so that I could spy on that new kid across the street. Every morning he looked taller. He seemed to grow an inch a day. Mom said he was probably going through a growth spurt. How come these growth spurts didn't happen to me? I wondered where I could pick one up. Too bad they didn't sell them at the store. I sure hoped that kid used up his growth spurt before next fall, or he'd probably take the spot I was trying out for on the basketball team. I was sure that there had to be more to it than a growth spurt though. I bet that kid did some sort of weird exercises at night or had some sort of medieval stretching machine in his attic. I'd find out soon enough if I had a telescope.

Mom moved her hands to measure a different section of the sky.

She was as excited about the astronomy club as I was about fishing or video games. I guess everyone likes something different. I once heard that Becky, the shy kid in my class, has a really weird mother. She likes to collect paper clips. I mean, how many different kinds of paper clips can there be? Wouldn't you get totally bored after a while? I guess you could make a paper-clip fishing pole or a paper-clip leash. It would be a pretty weak leash though. It would probably do for a hamster or something, but I don't remember seeing too many hamsters with leashes. Maybe I could add that to my invention list. Then there's Jake's mom. She likes to collect garbage. Well, not all garbage. Just the kind that you can make art with, like foam trays and old cans. I caught her going through our recycling box twice last year.

I shook my head as I imagined Becky's mom and her paper-clip necklace and Jake's mom and her garbage art. Nope, having a mom who was interested in the stars was a whole lot better than having one who was fascinated by that other weird stuff.

I decided to tell Mom about my speech topic. I was right in the middle of describing things that weren't there when a giant pine cone hit me smack in the middle of my forehead. Maybe it was reminding me not to think too hard.

I looked up at the pine tree way above my head.

"Gravity," Mom said, laughing. "It's an unseen force."

"Things that aren't there!" we both said at once.

I nodded again and looked at the stars. I stretched my hand out in front of me and squinted. Maybe this astronomy thing wasn't so bad after all. I'd found another idea for my speech. Plus I'd learned a new trick of measuring. I wondered how many fingers wide Tiffany's brain was. I didn't think there could be anything that small. Maybe an atom. But it wasn't there. Or was it?

Chapter Eight

I didn't think about my speech again until Sunday. Sometimes chores, like returning video games or finding baseball gloves, get in the way of real life. By the time I'd conquered the last level in the new game I rented on Sunday afternoon, it was time to go fishing. Sam and I had decided to go fishing on Sunday instead of Monday this week. Sam thought I should use Monday and Tuesday nights to practice my speech, since I'd be giving it on Wednesday. Like I said, he always looks out for me. What a guy.

The problem was, I couldn't very well practice something that wasn't there. I still had only two lines to my speech. So far my speech was a thing that wasn't there. Somehow I didn't think Miss Steane would appreciate the joke.

"I saw this guy on TV who said he could see people's auras," Sam said as we settled down on the bank of the creek.

I dumped my half of the worms into my shoe this time and gave Sam the carton. "You mean like the aurora borealis?" I asked. I knew that was a fancy name for the northern lights. Mom's astronomy lectures were beginning to rub off on me.

"No," Sam corrected. "Every living thing is supposed to have this energy that surrounds it. Some people claim they can see it around people's bodies like shimmering lights and colors. You kind of have to squint to see it. You can't prove it's there or it's not there. It's really quite interesting."

Sam saw me yawn. "I guess you have to have an open mind," he apologized.

My mind was open—wide open. Ideas just flew right out of it before they had a chance to stick.

We spent the next ten minutes squinting at the trees across the stream to see if we could see their auras. I saw an old blue kite stuck in the top of the trees. I saw the squirrels racing across the branches.

Mainly what I saw was a bunch of ants trying to find something to eat.

That reminded me of the party on Wednesday. "Mom's punch is going to score some points with the Lamp's mother," I told Sam. "I even like it, even though it's good for me, so I can just imagine what she's going to think."

"Do you want some help making it?" Sam asked.

Normally I would let someone else do the work, but I wanted to handle this one on my own. Besides, it was straightforward. I knew the recipe was for eight people. There were twenty-four of us in the class, so Sam told me I would just have to multiply it by three. I was sure most of the ingredients were already at home. Even I couldn't possibly mess this one up.

Even though I'm not great at multiplying, I am pretty good at subtracting. I don't know why. I guess it's because I'm used to counting down the days until summer vacation or Christmas holidays. I had three nights to finish and practice my speech. Take one night away because of the baseball game on TV tonight. That left two nights. If I forced myself, I could probably manage to write two lines a night. Two nights, two lines each. Four lines. Hmmm. I doubted I could win the trophy with that.

Then I remembered the two lines I had already written. That would make six lines altogether. Six whole lines. Yep, I felt a lot better after that. A whole lot better. So good, in fact, that I almost forgot about my dentist appointment the next morning. Almost.

Chapter Nine

I don't know why I hate the dentist so much. It's not that I can't take the pain of the needle or drill, because I really am the toughest guy on the baseball team. I don't back down from anyone, not even the mean pitcher on the Wildcat team, who has to be at least eight feet tall. Last year I even played one game with a sprained ankle. We won.

It's just that when you're at the dentist's, you don't know what's in store for you. At least when you have a cavity you know what you're in for. It's the checkups I hate. You never know what's going to happen at a checkup. They could say, "Everything looks great. Good work." At least that's what they say in my dreams. I don't hear those words too much in real life.

With me it's usually silence and then someone says, "Tsk, tsk." They scribble something down on their charts and say, "We'll have to take care of that." That's a nice way of saying, "We'll have to stick a needle in your mouth and drill half your tooth away."

It's not knowing if those stupid little cavities are there or not that bugs me. I wish I knew before I went into the office. I guess they're sort of like the stuff on my speech list. Are they there or aren't they? This time I was pretty sure they would come under the category "Things That Are There."

I don't like the look of the dentist office. I don't even like the way it smells—like cleaning fluid or vinegar. And I really don't like the dentist's hands. Why do dentists always seem to have fat fingers? I guess it's so they can grab the giant needle and gigantic drill better.

Dr. Plain—or Dr. Pain, as I call him—gave my teeth one final pick and took his big hand out of my mouth.

There was silence. I listened to myself breathing.

"Tsk, tsk," he said. "It's just a small cavity, but we'll have to take care of that."

How did I know he was going to say that?

I must have looked at him like a caged animal because he patted me on the shoulder and said, "How about we do that right now?"

Good old Dr. Pain. He knows I don't like to think about coming to the dentist. He knows I'd rather just get it over with right then and there. Besides, like I said, it's not the actual filling that I hate. It's the checkups.

"We'll just do a quick X-ray to make sure everything else is okay," he said.

I thought about an X-ray as he put some cardboard wedges in my mouth. I was pretty sure they might be things that weren't there, so I asked Dr. Pain.

"X-rays are a type of radiation, just like light," he explained. "Our eyes can see normal light, but we can't see the shorter wavelength of X-rays. We use X-rays to make these films, and then we can see if you have any more hidden cavities."

Great. Just what I needed. I didn't really want to find out if I had any more cavities. Besides, I had kind of already guessed that I had one today. It must have been that ESP thing. ESP was another thing that either might or might not be there. I knew that ESP meant that you knew something was going to happen before it happened. I remembered once when I had known what hockey card was on top of the pack before I even opened it. It might have been a good guess. Maybe not though. And today I had known that I was going to have a cavity before I even got to the office. I guess the way my tooth had been aching for a month might have given it away.

I had way too many ideas swirling around my head. It was bad enough being upside down in that chair, let alone having to think about ideas for my speech. Two bad things in one day. The dentist and schoolwork. Two bad things too many. Do bad things come in threes?

Dr. Pain came back into the room. I squinted my eyes to try and see his aura. Sam had said that blue was the color of peace and calm. I could have used some peace and calm right then. Maybe if I concentrated hard enough he'd be blue. I squinted harder. The only good thing about the squinting business was that it made it a lot harder to see the needle.

Chapter Ten

My mouth was still numb when I got back to school after lunch. My mind pretty much went numb too when I started listening to Tiffany's speech.

"Etiquette describes the way we should interact with each other. It's all about politeness," Tiffany began. "Did you know that you should wait to start eating until your host unfolds her napkin and puts it on her lap? That you should only blot your mouth gently with your napkin and then put it back immediately? Nobody likes a messy eater," she said, looking at me.

Blah, blah, blah, I thought as I drew a fish on my hand. The Lamp was the last one to speak today, but definitely the most boring. One guy talked about helicopters and one girl babbled on about her baby sister.

I couldn't wait to get out of there. Luckily I'm good at tuning out annoying noise. I just pretend I'm in my video game battling the dragons in their supersonic jets.

After what seemed to be about a week, she finished. "Sometimes etiquette just can't be learned," she said, glaring at me. "Sometimes people are just too rude to listen."

The class clapped politely. I yawned. My hands were sore from all that writing the night before.

"See—everyone liked my speech," Tiffany said as she pushed past me on the way out of the school. "Please and thank you go a long way. You should learn what they mean."

"You're right," I said. "Would you please excuse me while I go and throw up? Thank you."

It's hard to be nice to Tiffany. My brain tells me to try, but sometimes my mouth just says what it wants to. It's like my mouth is its own boss. I'm kind of proud of that. I mean, when it comes right down to it, sometimes a big mouth comes in more handy than a big brain. You couldn't just use your brain to yell at your teammate to steal second when the catcher suddenly fumbles the ball. And what about if we were attacked by giant tarantulas? Your mouth would sure come in handy when you were screaming for help.

That night I added two more lines to my speech. It now had four lines.

Miss Steane, honorable judges, and fellow classmates,
Do you ever wonder if something is really there?
Like how a dog can hear a really high whistle?
We don't think that whistle's there, but it really is.

I was sweating. Writing was such hard work. I had two more lines though. I was really proud of myself now.

I didn't sleep much that night because I kept thinking about black holes and wormholes. Sam had said something about a wormhole being like a secret passageway out there in the universe. Things could sort of move through space and time all at once. Wouldn't that make it quicker for UFOS to get to us?

I put my head under the pillow. Some things are just better left unthought.

Chapter Eleven

On Tuesday morning the speeches continued. Most of them were pretty boring—famous authors and not-so-famous explorers—but at least they passed the time so that we didn't have to do real work like math.

Sam gave his speech on medieval times in the afternoon. It was pretty good except for the sentences he repeated three times. I guess he was pretty excited.

He brought in some props, like this catapult that he made. You could launch real stones with it and throw them right across the room. I wished he'd launch one at the fire alarm so that we could get out of school early.

Everybody clapped after Sam's speech. I did too. My hands weren't as sore as they had been the day before after Tiffany's speech. It's funny how they have a mind of their own too.

Becky did her speech next. It was about ventriloquism. She even brought in a real dummy that she had borrowed from her uncle. The only problem was she got so nervous that she forgot to move the dummy's mouth. A talking dummy who doesn't talk kind of misses the point.

I felt sorry for Becky. It looked like she was going to start crying. Tiffany rolled her eyes at her and turned the other way. I gave Becky the thumbs-up and clapped really hard. I don't know why some people get so nervous about giving a speech. Then again, I guess having Tiffany rolling her eyes at you from the front row would give anyone the creeps.

"Are you ready for tomorrow?" Sam asked as we headed home after school.

"Sure," I lied. "The speech will be easy."

"What about the punch?" Sam was always worrying about me. I guess he needed someone to worry about besides himself. I didn't mind helping him out with that.

"Yeah, yeah," I said. "I've got everything I need."

I hoped everything I needed was in the kitchen cupboards, which are full of organic this and organic that. Mom was out at another astronomy meeting. That was good because I wanted to surprise her by making the punch myself. I looked at the recipe.

Organic Smoothie Delight
1 cup organic grape juice
2 cups organic cranberry juice
1 cup organic orange juice
2 cups organic iced tea
3 tsp organic honey
2 tsp organic flaxseed oil
½ cup organic soy milk

I did some quick calculations in my head. Sam had said that I needed to multiply everything by three to make enough for the class. Something didn't seem to add up though. I definitely didn't have all the ingredients.

I decided to go down to the grocery store on the corner and get what I needed. I counted out some of my paper route money that I'd been saving for a new video game. I hated to let it go, but it was worth it. I could just see the look on Mom's face when Mrs. Wilson raved about how good the punch was. She would be so happy. She could thank me later. I had just enough money left over for a gigantic bottle of root beer. Root beer helps me think. I like to see how many thoughts I can think before I burp. I knew I'd need help thinking if I was going to work on my speech that night.

On the way out of the store, I ran into Mrs. Wilson. It must have been ESP again because I had just been thinking about her. When I say "ran into her," I really mean "ran into her." She knocked me right over. Her purse fell on the ground and everything spilled out. I scrambled to my feet and began to pick up her things.

"Hmpf," she snorted, looking down at me like I was a pesky mosquito or an annoying fly. "Watch where you're going next time, Anison."

I didn't bother correcting her. I figured not getting my name right ran in the family.

"Sorry, Mrs. Wilson." I handed her purse back to her. "That's a real nice wallet you've got there."

Mrs. Wilson snorted again.

"It's sort of like my Mom's wallet," I continued. "She's got an extra-nice one to keep her grocery money in. She needs it with all her fancy recipes and stuff."

Mrs. Wilson snorted one more time and left. I guess compliments didn't work with her kind. The punch would have to speak for itself.

When I got home I put the punch ingredients out on the table. I measured and I mixed. I mixed and I measured. I must have made extra-strong iced tea, because the punch looked darker than Mom's. It sure looked tasty though. If I hadn't had to finish my root beer so I could burp, I would have had a glass of it. I gave it one final stir. At last my masterpiece was done. Now I had to finish my speech.

I thought and I wrote. I wrote and I thought. Before I went to bed that night I added two more lines to my speech. I now had six lines. That would have to do.

Miss Steane, honorable judges, and fellow classmates,
Do you ever wonder if something is really there?
Like how a dog can hear a really high whistle?
We don't think that whistle's there, but it really is.
Black holes, wormholes, atoms and ghosts.
With an open mind, you can see the most.

I especially liked that rhyming bit. That would prove to Miss Steane that I'd been listening to the poetry stuff we'd learned earlier in the year. I'd saved it till now to show her just how good I was. If I didn't win the speech contest, maybe I could enter the poetry contest next year.

Right now my speech was done. Well, the six lines that I needed were written, anyway. I could just fill in the blanks tomorrow. I could make those six sentences turn into sixty or six hundred or even six thousand if I wanted to. As long as I had the bare bones of what I needed I would be fine. Why would anybody waste their energy writing down every word they were going to say? They should learn to trust themselves to come up with the right words at the right time, like I did.

I knew I needed to speak for three minutes. I'd throw in a thing or two about gravity and ESP too.

I would just add things as I went. After all, my nickname wasn't Add for nothing. My brain was good at stuff like that. I was sure of it. The only thing I wasn't one hundred percent sure about was my mouth. Like I said, sometimes my mouth is its own boss.

Chapter Twelve

Wednesday morning at school just flew past. Do you ever notice that when you want time to go slowly it speeds up? Like it's getting back at you for wasting it. I really needed that time to practice my speech. Or at least my six lines of it anyway.

At lunch we set up the food for the party in the party room. It was really the study room for the grade fives and sixes, but we called it the party room. I guess we were supposed to feel honored to have our own study room. "Party room" sounded a heck of a lot better to me. I mean, why would you waste a perfectly good room on studying?

Everybody laid out their snacks for the party afterwards. I put my punch out smack in the middle of the table. It still looked a lot darker than Mom's version, but maybe it was just the lighting in there. It sort of reminded me of the color of mud at the creek on a rainy day.

Mrs. Wilson showed up for the afternoon. She promptly moved my punch out of the way and put Tiffany's peanut butter cookies in the center of the table. Like daughter, like mother. She even shoved aside the ventriloquist's dummy that Becky had used for her speech the day before. It must be pretty bad when you think a dummy is going to compete with your daughter for attention. Then again, it's Tiffany we're talking about. The dummy would win hands down.

Miss Steane put the money we'd collected for the pizza in a bowl by the punch. She turned out the lights and closed the door. She told us that we weren't allowed to go back in there until after the speeches were done and the pizza delivered. Then we could have our party.

I was the last person to give my speech. I pretended to listen to the other speeches that afternoon, but really my mind was just racing. It was racing so fast that I couldn't catch it. I kept reminding myself that I already had the six lines memorized, and that it would be easy to make up the rest. I'd just pretend I was talking to Sam, telling him some made-up story about fishing or baseball…

All I needed to do was fill in the blanks for three minutes. The problem was I couldn't really fill in the blanks when my whole mind was a blank. There was nothing to fill in. For some reason I couldn't seem to concentrate on my speech. It must have been the chocolate bars I had at lunch. Mom had told me that too much sugar would give me a sugar rush. I wished the sugar would rush to my brain and give it a kick start.

After recess, Mrs. Wilson came storming into the classroom, raving about how somebody had snuck into the party room and helped themselves to some snacks and some of my punch, which was now spilled all over the cookies and Becky's dummy's head. There was also some money gone from the pizza bowl. I was sure Mrs. Lamp was more worried about Tiffany's precious cookies than the missing money.

"Someone in here has been in the party room," Mrs. Wilson growled, staring straight at me. Why does everyone automatically think that if something's messed up, it's me who did it? I guess I should be proud of myself for having people think I'm so powerful, but sometimes I get tired of being the first one to be accused.

Miss Steane put on her sternest teacher voice. "All right, class. Whoever is responsible for taking the food and money, please own up to it right now. Don't let this ruin our party."

There was silence as everyone squirmed. Nobody volunteered any information.

Mrs. Wilson snarled, "We'll find out who the thief is. There's a way to find out. There's always a way. We'll just look for the evidence. It will show up. That student is going to pay." She glared at every one of us, stopping extra long on me.

I felt sorry for whoever did it. With Detective Lamp on the case, they wouldn't stand a chance.

"We'll discuss this matter after the speeches are done," Miss Steane said firmly. "Right now, let's have the last two speakers."

Chris, the guy in front of me, gave his speech on whales. I pretended to listen. I should have been using that time to go over my own speech, but I couldn't help thinking about Becky's dummy instead. I could just imagine what it looked like with my punch all over it. Poor Becky would be really upset now. I'd have to give her some of Mom's extra paper clips to take home to her mother, who was probably going to be mad. I heard the class clap. Chris took a bow. My hands started to sweat.

"And finally, we have Addison Addley and *The Things That Aren't There.*" I heard Miss Steane speak, as if from another planet. Everything seemed very far away.

I'm really glad that my legs have a mind of their own because they somehow found their way to the front of the classroom.

Everyone was quiet. They just stared at me, waiting for something. Then I remembered they were waiting for me to speak.

I coughed. I blinked. I started my speech.

Chapter Thirteen

"Miss Steane, honorable judges, and fellow classmates, do you ever wonder if something is really there?"

I coughed again. I blinked again. The class waited. They waited some more. I heard someone blow his nose.

I couldn't remember a thing. My mind was suddenly as empty as a black hole. The Lamp's mother must have thrown off my brilliant memorization skills. I wiped the sweat off my forehead.

I thought hard. The harder I thought, the farther those six lines ran away from me.

After a couple more seconds of dead silence, some wise guy at the back of the class started clapping. A couple more kids started giggling.

I saw Sam trying to urge me on. He put his fingers in his mouth like he was going to whistle.

"Oh yeah," I said, breathing a sigh of relief. "Like how a dog whistles really high."

Everyone laughed and then looked at me as if I was a complete moron. Which I was beginning to think I was. Everyone knows dogs can't whistle.

"Some people believe in microwaves," I stumbled on. Now that was even more stupid.

Why couldn't I remember anything? It felt as if those six lines had suddenly decided to take a vacation. Even if I had remembered them, I realized that I didn't actually know much about any of the things on my list. I guess I should have paid just a bit more attention to Sam and my mom and the dentist. Just this once.

"Sometimes ghosts fall out of the sky because of gravity," I said. That's all I could think of to say on that topic. It's hard to talk about something you don't even like to think about.

Everyone continued to stare at me like I was a lunatic.

There were words in the back of my brain. They just didn't seem to come together properly. Sort of like how numbers never seem to come together properly for me. I knew there was something about black holes, but for the life of me I couldn't remember what a black hole was. I wished I could crawl into a black hole right then and there.

I scrunched up my eyes to try to jog my brain into action. I ground my teeth together. My teeth, X-rays ….

"Oh yeah, dentists use X-rays to find black holes in your teeth," I said. "Sometimes they use ESP too."

Everybody looked as confused as I felt. Now I felt confused *and* stupid. That's not a great combination. This was getting ridiculous. I had to make some sort of sense about at least one thing on my list.

I could talk about wormholes. I knew wormholes had something to do with time travelling and secret passageways, but I couldn't remember what. I wished that I could time-travel out of the classroom to another planet right then and there. I wouldn't even care if a whole team of aliens in UFOs came to get me.

I saw Tiffany sneering at me from her front-row desk. She yawned and went cross-eyed. She put her fingers in her mouth like she was trying to gag. I knew I had to think fast. At the very least, I knew I had to talk fast.

That was it. Finally I knew what I had to do. I'd have to rely on my trusty old mouth instead of my not-so-trusty brain. I'd start with wormholes.

I took a deep breath and let my mouth run wild.

"How many people here like fishing?" I started.

A few people put up their hands.

"Well, do you ever go fishing and forget the bait?" I asked the class. "Then you don't know what to do. You decide to look around for some worms, but you don't see any. But you do see these little hills and lines of dirt. You're happy because you know that there must be worms around, because something had to have made those little wormholes. You see, you can't see the worms, but you know they're there because of the holes. They're things that aren't there, but they really are."

I looked at Sam for support. He looked like he was going to strangle me after class. He'd spent all that time researching the topic, and I had just thrown it out the window. He shook his head and then scratched his nose and shook his head again. He must have been even more nervous than me.

I was on a roll now. I remembered there was something about atoms.

"Remember last year when we almost lost the baseball tournament?" I continued. "Well, what saved us was our lucky charm. It was Adam's little green plastic frog. We'd won every game before that when he wore it under his hat, but he lost it just before the tournament. We thought we were done for sure."

I didn't bother telling the class that the frog wasn't really lost. I had borrowed it to try to scare Tiffany, but I'd decided to flush it down the toilet instead for an experiment.

"Anyway, we imagined that we still had Adam's frog for good luck. We concentrated and pretended it was there, just under his hat. We pretended it was there for the whole game. It worked. We won the tournament. It was all because of something that wasn't there, but we imagined it was."

Atoms, Adam's, what's the difference? They were close enough. Wow, I was good, if I did say so myself.

Miss Steane had her eyes shut as if she didn't know what to think. Either that or she had a really bad headache.

Some of the kids were nodding. That was a good sign. I think. By now Sam looked like steam was coming out of his nose. I thought he was going to blow up.

I looked at my watch. About one minute had gone by. I had two more to go.

I shouldn't have looked down at my watch because that seemed to stop my mouth.

Now both my brain and my mouth were quiet. Too quiet. I started to feel panicky again, but suddenly I remembered auras.

"Listen," I whispered. "Look around you really carefully and sort of squint like this." I showed them how to do it. "If you kind of go a bit cross-eyed, you can see weird colors around people." I tried to sound as mysterious as I could. "There's some sort of stuff that comes out of them, some sort of energy or something."

I blabbed on for a whole minute about colors and what they meant. I told them how there were many different shades of the same color, so one color could mean different things. Blue was calm and peaceful. Red was sometimes energetic but sometimes nervous. I wondered if anybody could see red around me right then. Of course, maybe they saw lavender, which was the color of imagination and daydreamers. I then stood very still and pretended I could see auras around people's heads. Everybody believed me. I saw everyone turn around and squint at each other.

Things were looking up. I'd bought some valuable time while they looked for auras. I scrambled, trying to think of something else to say.

It was then that the weirdest thing happened. I really did see my first aura. At least I thought I did.

"For example, look at Tiffany," I began excitedly. "She's got this greenish color around her." I swear I could actually see it. Maybe Sam had been right about this aura stuff. The problem was, it wasn't just around her body like it was supposed to be. It was actually on her. On her face, to be exact.

"Look at her," I urged the rest of the class. "An aura is something that isn't there, but it really could be. Concentrate hard and you'll see the stuff coming out of Tiffany."

Everybody turned to stare at Tiffany. I couldn't believe the Lamp's face might actually save my speech. It was usually red and shiny, but now it was definitely grayish green and damp. It was getting greener and damper by the second.

The Lamp raised her hand.

"Not now, Tiffany," Miss Steane said. "We're in the middle of a speech. It's rude to interrupt it."

That was nice of Miss Steane, but for once I wished she had given Tiffany what she wanted. No sooner had she put her hand down than she bolted up from her desk, took two steps toward me and threw up the most disgusting stream of liquid I'd ever seen.

It was brown, like the color of mud at the creek on a rainy day. About one and a half cups of it, I reckon.

Chapter Fourteen

Everyone gasped as Tiffany flew out of the room with the disgusting junk dripping from her mouth.

Miss Steane ran after her but came back to the class in a couple of seconds.

"Mrs. Wilson has taken Tiffany to get cleaned up," she said. "Let's all try to settle down and hear the end of the speech. We're sorry for the interruption, Addison."

"No problem," I said. Heck, it was great. I'd have to thank the Lamp after school for throwing up. I guess she was telling the truth—I really did make her sick. Miss Steane had said that we could use props to make our speech better. I couldn't think of a better prop than that.

Besides, it had given me a few extra seconds to think. My brain kicked in at last.

Without Tiffany in the room, those lines decided to come back from vacation.

Black holes, wormholes, atoms and ghosts.
With an open mind, you can see the most.

I bowed. The class clapped, real clapping this time, not the polite stuff.

Miss Steane looked at her watch. "It's a few seconds short, but I guess that's understandable since you were probably thrown off by Tiffany."

Like I said before, I like Miss Steane. I wouldn't go so far as to say that I liked Tiffany, but she'd sure come in handy today. I couldn't have timed her green face any better if I had tried myself. Which, of course, I wouldn't have.

After Miss Steane recorded her marks, we all voted for our favorite speech. I voted for Becky.

Miss Steane counted up the votes. We all held our breath. I thought for sure that Becky would win because everyone felt sorry for her. As long as it wasn't Tiffany I didn't really care.

Miss Steane looked surprised. "This year's contest was close," she said, "but we have a winner. I have to admit that it was a strange but interesting speech. The favorite speech trophy goes to Addison Addley for *The Things That Aren't There*," she announced with a half-smile. She probably didn't want to look too happy for me, even though she was.

I couldn't believe that I had actually won! As I said before, sometimes a big mouth is as handy as a big brain.

I accepted the trophy from Miss Steane and took a big bow. The trophy was a cup with two little handles and a plaque. I would have preferred a gold medal or something I could sell later on, but winners can't be choosy.

I don't like to brag, but maybe I really did deserve the trophy. Miss Steane had said that the speech had to be entertaining, and, boy, had I been entertaining. Well, at least my special effects had been. I guess everybody had enjoyed watching Tiffany throw up. It sure beat listening to the history of industrialization or learning how to be polite. I guess Tiffany had learned something from her own speech though. After all, she had tried to excuse herself politely before she got sick.

I was just about to take another bow when Mrs. Wilson stormed into the class. She practically ran right at me.

"What did you put into that punch?" she yelled.

The punch? Mom's prize-winning punch? What did that have to do with anything?

Then I remembered the stream of stuff coming out of Tiffany's mouth. She must have been drinking it. That would explain the mud brown color she had spit out. What I couldn't understand was why it would have made her sick. It was Mom's prize-winning punch. Everybody liked it.

"Answer me," the Lamp's mother continued to yell. I didn't know why she was so upset. If her daughter hadn't been so greedy, none of this would have happened.

"I followed a recipe," I explained. At this point I didn't want to tell her it was Mom's recipe. I had the feeling Mrs. Wilson wasn't too impressed by the punch.

I fumbled around in my pocket. "Here. See for yourself," I said, handing her a crumpled piece of paper with some used gum on it. I pulled off the gum to save for later.

Miss Steane took the recipe from the Lamp's mother. She smoothed it out and read the list of ingredients and instructions. "Are you sure you followed the recipe exactly, Addison?" she asked.

"Yeah, I multiplied everything by three to get enough for the class," I said proudly. "I didn't even use my calculator." Miss Steane read the list back to me.

1 cup organic grape juice x 3 = 3 cups
2 cups organic cranberry juice x 3 = 6 cups
1 cup organic orange juice x 3 = 3 cups
2 cups organic iced tea x 3 = 6 cups
3 tsp organic honey x 3 = 9 tsp
2 tsp organic flaxseed oil x 3 = 6 tsp
½ cup organic soy milk x 3 = 3 ½ cups

"Three-and-a-half cups?" Miss Steane asked. "That's wrong, Addison. One half cup times three is three half cups or one-and-a-half cups. It's not three-and-a-half cups. You put in far too much soy milk."

Did I mention that I can't multiply very well? Especially fractions? Sometimes those pesky numbers just get mixed up. Like I said before, fractions sometimes have a disgusting way of catching up to you.

I couldn't think of anything more disgusting than what had come out of Tiffany's mouth.

Miss Steane was frowning. "That doesn't explain why the punch was so dark or why it would make Tiffany sick," she said. "You had way too much soy milk but Tiffany's not allergic to soy products—no one in the class is."

"But I didn't have too much soy milk," I said with a smile.

If there's one thing I'm good at, it's switching things around. I hadn't been able to find any soy milk at the corner grocery store, so I had found something just like it instead. Well, maybe not just like it, but close.

"Don't worry about the soy milk," I explained. "I didn't put any in. I substituted that other soy stuff instead." I was proud of myself.

"What other stuff?" Miss Steane asked slowly.

"You know—the stuff we put on Chinese food. Soy sauce." Milk, sauce, what's the difference? They were both made of soy.

Mrs. Wilson looked like she was going to strangle me. Her eyes bulged out of her head even more than Tiffany's. "You mean to say that you put three-and-a-half cups of soy *sauce* in that punch? No wonder my baby got sick!"

I didn't see what the big deal was.

Tiffany came back into the classroom. She didn't look sick anymore, except for the brown stuff on her shirt. Her face was shiny and red, just the way it always was. She looked like she was going to kill me.

I coughed politely, the way Tiffany had taught us.

"Um, aren't you forgetting something?" I pointed out. "When did Tiffany get a chance to drink my punch? She must have been the one who broke into the party room at recess. The proof is on her shirt." And in her stomach, I added to myself. Or at least it had been.

I grinned. Success was sweet. Mrs. Wilson had been right about one thing: Look for the evidence. It will show up. It always does.

Chapter Fifteen

Sam and I had a celebratory fishing trip at the creek that night. I took the trophy with me. After all, it wasn't every day that I actually won something.

Sam slapped me on the back. "You did really well today, really good, really well!" he said. He was practically bubbling over with excitement. "Thanks to you, we still got to have our party."

It really had been a good party. It seems that innocent little Tiffany hadn't been so innocent after all. She had snuck into the party room and helped herself to some punch and cookies. Then she had helped herself to some money too. She was going to use it to bribe her friends to vote for her speech. Instead she had to put the money back and promise to pay for cleaning Becky's dummy. She also had to apologize to the class.

We got to have our pizza and a dance too. The only person I would have danced with was Becky's dummy, but it smelled too much like my punch. Tiffany just sat in the corner and glared at everyone. I guess she felt stupid because she'd been caught in the act. She knew she'd screwed up, but she'd hated apologizing.

I slept really well that night. There was something about watching Tiffany get what she deserved that made me feel kind of nice and sleepy, like the way I felt after I drank chamomile tea once when I was sick.

I was surprised to see Mrs. Wilson waiting outside the classroom the next day after school. It wasn't a great way to end my day.

She demanded an apology from me. From me? What had I done wrong? All I'd done was make a little mistake with my fractions. And one of the ingredients. They were honest mistakes. I mean, who really cares if ½ times 3 is 1 ½ instead of 3 ½ ? Well, except for Tiffany. Her stomach cared. She shouldn't have been so greedy in the first place. She was the one who'd gulped down the punch when she wasn't even supposed to have been in that room. It wasn't fair that I had to apologize.

"Well, we're waiting," Mrs. Wilson said, tapping her big foot in its pointed brown shoe. Tiffany had popped up beside her.

I swallowed hard and stared at Mrs. Wilson's big foot. I thought about her sitting at the table in the astronomy club room, tapping her big hand before she voted for the new positions on the board. I thought about black holes and wormholes and things that weren't there, like how I wished I weren't there right then. I decided to take one for the team.

"Sorry, Tiffany," I mumbled to the floor.

Tiffany smiled a slow, sweet smile. "What was that?" she asked.

I cleared my throat and said it again. "Sorry."

"And here," I said quickly, before I changed my mind. I pulled the favorite speech trophy out of my backpack and shoved it at her. "You take this. You deserve it."

It was just a dumb cup. I didn't need it. I knew I had really won the competition. Sometimes you've just gotta do what you've gotta do.

"Well then," Mrs. Wilson muttered, not knowing what to say. She smiled at me, a real smile, not even a fake one.

Tiffany's face lit up like a lamp. For a second, just one tiny second, I kind of felt sorry for her. She really wanted that trophy. It must have meant a lot to her. Sort of like what winning the baseball tournament last year had meant to me.

That feeling only lasted for a second because then she scrunched up her face into a twisted sneer again. "Thanks, Oddison," the Lamp purred. "I'm going to go home and have a victory drink in this with some real punch. Victory. You don't know what that word means, do you?" she whispered to me as she strode away.

Victory. Oh yeah, I knew what that word meant. It was sweet. I thought of Tiffany heading home with her trophy. I thought about her pouring some of her own precious punch into it. I thought about her gulping it down. I thought about how my half of the worms had been sitting in that trophy last night at the creek. Oh yeah, victory was sweet.

Chapter Sixteen

I studied the pages in front of me. Ever since Mom had found out that I'd failed my last chapter review in math, she'd found even more ways for me to look at numbers. She said she thought I could use a little practice. More than a little practice, if you ask me.

I was now in charge of the household budget. Mom just didn't get it. With me in charge, we'd be broke in a week. Luckily I was only going to be in charge for a month.

"You know, Mom, if you'd cut back on all of that organic stuff from the health food store, we'd have more money for other food," I suggested. More real food, like ice cream with chocolate syrup and green sprinkles. You could never have too much of that stuff lying around the house.

Mom grinned at me. "Nice try, Einstein." She put down her cup of green tea. "You know, speaking of organic food, I saw Mrs. Wilson coming out of the health food store yesterday. Maybe she's turning into a health nut like me. I think I'll give her the recipe for my organic fruit punch at the next meeting. I bet she'd really enjoy that."

I coughed up my peppermint tea.

"Yeah, well, you might want to hold off on that," I said. Mom still didn't know about the punch disaster. No use getting her upset or anything. She'd just been elected to the treasurer position. It had been a close call, five votes to four. I wondered which way good old Mrs. Wilson had voted. I'd made her daughter sick, but then again I'd made her daughter happy by giving her that trophy. Maybe one deed cancelled out the other—like multiplying fractions.

I had to think fast. "She was probably just there to put up flyers for the school fundraiser," I said. It could have been true. There really was going to be a fundraiser, and Mrs. Wilson was sure to be in charge of it.

"I bet she's not interested in that organic stuff at all," I continued. "Actually, I'm pretty sure of it. I heard her say she wouldn't touch that organic stuff if you paid her to. She says it's a total waste of money." I didn't mention the fact that Mrs. Wilson had only been talking about the punch. Some things are better left unsaid.

"Well, keep working on those numbers and see if we can cut some corners," Mom said as she headed out the back door. "I'm going to go take a peek at the stars. I can't wait to borrow the telescope at the next meeting!" She practically floated outside.

Great. A telescope. Old starlight. Black holes. Wormholes.

Just what I needed. That's how this whole mess started in the first place, looking for things that weren't there. Maybe I could talk Mom into buying a new video game with spaceships and aliens instead. She'd have lots of stars to look at then.

I finished up the page I was working on and went upstairs to bed. Boy, was I tired. My brain wasn't used to working that hard. I was sure I'd be seeing numbers all night in my sleep.

Maybe I could get Sam to help me out the next day. I'd come up with a really incredible plan to make this number stuff easier. Heck, that budget would practically write itself. After all, I'd already proven that two heads are better than one.

I turned on the tap to brush my teeth. I gave them a quick scrub. I did my usual thing. I was just going to shut off the water when I decided to brush them a little longer, just this once. Who knows, just because I couldn't see those disgusting little germs, it didn't mean that they weren't really there. They might be just like dog whistles and wormholes. Like I said before, you've got to have an open mind about these things. Or at least half of one.

Melody DeFields McMillan grew up in the countryside in southwestern Ontario and now lives in Simcoe, not far from where she grew up. As well as being a writer, she is a teacher and the mother of a daughter and a son. When she isn't writing, she is enjoying nature.

Feather Brain

Maureen Bush

978-1-55143-877-1
$7.95 • 136 pp

Ten Thumb Sam

Rachel Dunstan Muller

978-1-55143-699-9
$7.95 • 128 pp

Racing for Diamonds

Anita Daher

978-1-55143-675-3
$7.95 • 128 pp

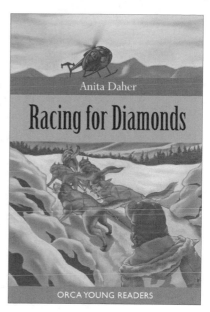

Lucky's Mountain

Diane Maycock

978-1-55143-682-1
$7.95 • 112 pp

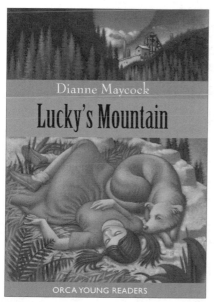

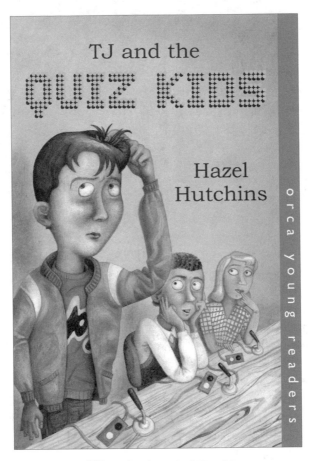

TJ series by Hazel Hutchins

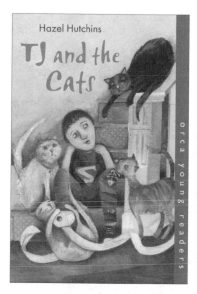

Hazel Hutchins

TJ and the Cats

orca young readers

TJ and the Haunted House

Hazel Hutchins

AN
ORCA
YOUNG READER

TJ and the Rockets

Hazel Hutchins

orca young readers

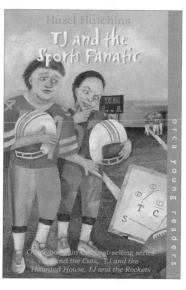

Hazel Hutchins

TJ and the Sports Fanatic

orca young readers

Other books in the best-selling series:
TJ and the Cats, TJ and the
Haunted House, TJ and the Rockets